LEGO CITY

NEED FOR SPEED!

By Trey King
Art by Chuck Primeau

SCHOLASTIC INC.

ISBN 978-0-545-62900-3

LEGO, the LEGO logo, the Brick and Knob configurations and the Minifigure are trademarks of the LEGO Group. © 2014 The LEGO Group. Produced by Scholastic Inc. under license from the LEGO Group.

12 11 10 9 8 7 6 5 4 3 2 1   14 15 16 17 18 19/0

Printed in the U.S.A.   40
First printing, January 2014
Designed by Angela Jun

LEGO® City is having a race! Anyone with wheels can join. There are race cars, monster trucks, and even a circus bear on a bicycle!

You ready to win?

There is something that many of the racers don't know. Two *cheaters* have entered the race—the terrible twins, Taylor and Tyler!

4

Taylor and Tyler set traps *before* the race.
They want to win, no matter what it takes.

Someone put a patch of glue on the road! This looks like the work of Taylor and Tyler.

The Auto Transporter gets stuck. Meanwhile, the other racers speed through the course.

MV60060

HJ60060

Luckily, the driver has an extra vehicle. He jumps into the top car and hits the gas!

But this car gets stuck in the glue, too. He is out of the race!

As Taylor and Tyler drive by, they laugh and wave. What a pair of meanies!

Taylor and Tyler also painted a fake sign. Most of the racers do not see it. Too bad for the drivers of the Tow Truck and Jet-Ski Transporter. They *do* see the sign. Oh, no!

THIS WAY

JM60058

They take the wrong turn onto the pier. Watch out for the fishermen!

The trucks end up on the coast guard's boat! Luckily, no one is hurt. And the Jet Skis come in handy. Instead of trying to finish the race, the drivers decide to cool off.

While Tyler drives, Taylor uses a rope to open the back of the logging truck. The logs spill everywhere.

Time for a traffic jam!

CRASH!

The Camper gets stuck behind all the logs.
What are they going to do?

The campers decide to have a picnic. They build a fire and make s'mores to share with their new friends.

The nails pop the tires. The cars spin in circles across the road.

Luckily, they make a safe landing—right onto a pile of pillows in the bed store.

The twins forgot to put gas in their truck. It looks like they might not win after all!

Too bad they forgot about some of the traps they set before the race.

So, why did the bear want to win the trophy?

The bear needed a bowl for ice cream.